15
STRANGERS

CONVERSATIONS THAT MEAN 'A LIFETIME'
STRANGERS ARE PART OF US, NOT DIFFERENT FROM US!

By
"RAAZ" DHEERAJ SHARMA

Published by InkQuills Publishing House
www.inkquills.in

First Edition 2020
All Rights Reserved.
Copyright © "Raaz" Dheeraj Sharma

ISBN: 978-81-948873-5-5

<u>ACKNOWLEDGEMENT</u>

I express my deed appreciation to the entire team at InkQuills Publishing House. You all have made publishing a wonderful experience for me.

Special Thanks to my thoughtful and competent Editor Ms. Preeti Priyadarshini for your wisdom and for your belief in this project.

I also express sincere gratitude to Ms. Kanudha Gupta and Ms. Ritanshi Jain, who have supported my work from day one.

Love and Respect to my parents, brother and sisters, who have encouraged me.

Lots of Love to My Friends who were with me while I was completing this book.

Thank You.

ABOUT THE AUTHOR

He loves to ponder in his thoughts and extract potentiality out of them. He is kind of mysterious, thoughtful person with logical thinking as a trait.

He feels, "life is beautiful and is well constructed in oceans of imagination. Also, the mind is like a tool of projection for imagination".

"Being a lawyer by profession, he understands the values of a decision holder and the indispensable power of a pen."

Life seems interesting and challenging at the same time. Here, he happily discusses the meetings and talks between strangers. Talk with Strangers is altogether a life-changing experience. They act as a mentor to all through their inseparable experiences. These stories will enrich his readers' mind with the encouragement of dwelling into beautiful beings, the next morning. Every time they'll open the book, they will feel enlightened.

He is here to share every bit of his knowledge and gained wisdom through experiences with his blessed audience. He feels learning together from others' experiences makes you transform into a better being. With this, he assures every closing chapter will embark life learnt lessons in your mind further improvising your life and making the world a better place for existence.

<u>EDITOR's NOTE</u>

"Amidst of strangers we grew stronger. Strangers are part of us, not different from us!"

Being a student and having a passion towards writing and editing I strongly believe every stranger out there has a role to play in our lives. Strangers are huge part of us, we meet them each day and all of them have a story and lesson to tell us.

This book exactly sums up what a stranger can teach you and how can they change your lives.

As you will go through the 15 different and unique chapters of this book, I assure you that every page of this book will definitely teach you something.

Talking about the author, he is an excellent person who sees the world in different sight and so he has poured his experiences in this book.

Once you go through the book you will realize how beautifully he describes incidents that were meant to be just normal.

This book aims to teach people that Strangers are part of our life and we have to remember them.

Preeti Priyadarshini

CONTENT

<u>To</u>

<u>My Readers</u>

Let's Start A New Journey

Preface

"Strangers are Terrestrial Wisdom Sources, known as experts in dictating the factual life occurrences in the form of beautifully crafted stories."

Kanudha Gupta

From the beginning, this book will make you travel into the conversations carried with 15 different strangers. The book will make you realize that everyone carries a story. Also, this book will act as a source of changing perceptions regarding talks with "unknown".

As you'll be clicking over the pages, you'll re-discover wisdom. For example, you'll be coming across conversations explaining time as a luxury of happiness, lending hands to help even on the disastrous points where help will be highlighted as a pleasure to internal joy, the third chapter will be the responsive mirror to the dark issues around, making realization and acceptance the king of the conversation, and so on. Every chapter has a moral to it which is indirectly an opportunity and this solely depends on us whether we'll gain something from it or just let it pass through.

As a reader, you'll also get to enjoy talks with Gabriella Wright, an actress and Suhail Mehraj, a Kashmiri Youth Activist laying their insights on problems dealing with mental health and depression.

"Strangers are part of us, not different from us!"

All the best, my dear readers. Let's travel together in search of wisdom in these real conversations which are exemplary.

Introduction

Although am not that good with numbers, but let's start with statistics. At this particular moment when am writing this, the overall population of this beautiful world is 7,773,930,376 and the numbers are increasing which is available at https://www.worldometers.info/world-population/ and am sure that now when you all are reading this, the numbers might look different and maybe it must have changed drastically. As we know world is big enough and we are a part of it. Maybe we are not in connection or in touch, directly or indirectly, with every individual of the World but still from morning to night, we are facing several unknown faces.

Large number of faces which we are facing or will have to face while crossing the roads, the streets, metros, offices and at other public places in our daily life are unknown to us. They are neither our relatives nor our friends. Even they are not our enemies. Then who are they? They all are unknown to us. They all are strangers.

Every face has its own story. They want to communicate; they want to share and they want to be with someone for some time so that they can freely share whatever they have in their mind as well as in their heart with someone unknown. To someone who is not going to judge them by listening to their stories. They want some kind of freedom and people get that when they interact with Strangers because they believe that there is no boundation, no formalities, no predetermined thoughts and no answerability and they don't have to explain everything to them.

I got the opportunity to meet with some beautiful souls who are strangers. But that does not mean who are known to me are not beautiful. All individuals in this planet are beautiful. It's just depends upon our perspective and on us that how we will see them and how we are going to judge them. Those who don't seem to be beautiful souls for us may be beautiful for others. That is the reason why I'm always saying and believe that we don't have any right to judge anyone. Even though when some individuals are not in regular touch with me, I can't just say that they are my enemies or they are somehow bad. It's possible that some other day we both took a wrong decision and there is scope of improvement and change which is the only permanent aspect of nature. So, this is for them- To all of the people, who were hurt because of my wrong decision, I am sending my unconditional apology to all of them. I am still trying to improve myself from yesterday to make a better tomorrow because we all have that opportunity to be better than yesterday and it's time to recognize that it is better to improve ourselves than making complaints about others or criticizing them to prove that you are right.

When I met unknown souls, I was able to know their stories, I started understanding their world and communicate with them and share my thoughts with them. But this is not the sole reason for writing about them. The prime reason of writing this is that I learned a lot from each and every stranger I met and from their stories which I heard. I learned about life, love and humanity as well as I learned their way of living life and about everything which is helping us to be a better human. And I am sharing those lessons of my life with you all; with the hope that you will learn something from their stories. Each and every stranger of our life are our teachers. It's upon us to be the student and learn from them or to treat them as another stranger of our life and ignore them.

To Senior Citizens: Time Is What You Can Give

"What Money Can't Buy Time Can."

Time is crucial for all of us, as we have a lot of work but don't have time to do all the things. Let's take a pause here and think about our life. Just think how many times we have used the line - "I don't have time". We don't have time to speak with our parents, relatives and friends. We don't have time to discover our hidden talents and hobbies. We don't have time to think about our life. We all are busy in our own illusional world. But what are we exactly doing?

I used to go for morning walk on winter days. And to be honest when i used to walk on those green grass it's feels something heavenly. Maybe you feel kind of alive again and that helps you to refresh yourself. While I was standing at one corner of the park to take off my shoes before placing my steps on those green grasses, I noticed an old man sitting. He was in white dress and his goggles kind of attracted me. He gave me a smile and his reactions were different from others who were there at the park, which compelled me to stop my walk at that moment. I went and sat next to him. I decided to spend some time with my new stranger.

I assumed from his appearance that he belonged to the Sikh community. *"Good Morning"* the old man who was looking more energetic than me greeted and I replied him by saying that *"Good Morning Ji"*. He was looking Great and he seemed to be in search of a person to speak his heart out with and I was there to speak with him. I could observe joy in his face.

Sometimes it's our duty to think about others happiness rather than thinking that we are wasting our time. Maybe by giving little time, we could give them happiness or some kind of satisfaction to them. Believe me, if they are more than 70-year-old and they are your relatives or some unknown senior citizen then I swear they have a lot to talk. They are always in search of someone to share their stories and topics with.

The old man shared some stories about Sikh Religion and I discussed about some religious books and stories with him. I enquired about his family. As well as he sang some beautiful songs but when I asked to record the song with my cell phone he denied. But after the discussion, he told me that "Nowadays no one has the patience to sit with us (he was referring old people) and listen to our thoughts." He further told me that even their family members have no time to talk. He added on that their grand-son and grand-daughter are too busy in their own life and if he asks something, they feel irritated and they think that he is trying to interfere in their life. But whereas he was trying to show care and love towards them.

At that time, I didn't have any explanation. I could feel his pain and as he was speaking this, he had tears in his eyes. Even today, I don't have any reason to disagree with his thoughts. In our country we have laws which are protecting senior citizens from violence and other stuffs. As we know all of them are not at old age homes. This is because parents who are turning into senior citizens are not making any complaint against their children due to bond called child love.

I am not saying that we all are responsible for this Or we should feel guilty for this, but somewhere we also have fault. What they all require is some of our time during which they can share their thoughts and share what they do daily.

He taught me that we can give happiness and satisfaction to anyone just by giving them some time. I didn't give anything to him but i just gave my time and sat with him and communicated with him. So basically what i did was I gave time to listen about his life experiences.

After talking with him, I concluded that yes we all are busy but we all are busy because we are not managing our time or maybe we don't even want to manage our time. We don't sit with any senior citizen thinking that there is a generation gap and they will not understand us or they are not capable to understand our life situations.

The only thing we all can do is give them time. We won't get anything in return but we all will definitely earn blessings from them. All I can suggest or say that give attention to them, just give your time and listen to their talks and listen whatever they want to share. Be humble and listen them patiently, cause that's what they really need.

Time is crucial but it's upon us how to manage it. Our mobile phones and friends are important but the smile on the face of any senior citizen is more valuable and beautiful than anything else. They need someone. They need us. Take a break and talk to them about their life. I am sure that you will get extreme satisfaction and relief after you do so.

She Is Not Your Toy, Don't Play With Her

"Woman are not toys; they need to be respected not the one to be played with."

Relationships are not any kind of agreements. We cannot treat them as Contract and we cannot apply the rule of contracts to break the relationships. Marriage is an important part of anyone's life and we all are incomplete without our life partner. Marriage is a bond between two souls that binds them with a cord of trust and love. But why do we see relationship falling apart and isn't love enough to keep the relationship strong?

It was during my internship days when I used to appear before Court for making request related to Passover or for taking adjournments or making submissions and taking dates in those matters which were listed under miscellaneous purposes. That was/is our prime duty during our internship. After completing my duty on that day in Court room, I was sitting in the canteen on third floor of Tis Hazari Courts for a cup of tea. That canteen is better than any other in Court Premises although I can't claim the same thing about tea however if you are an advocate or intern or client then you can have coffee from that place and I am sure that you will love a cup of coffee.

"Kya mein Yahan Baith Sakti Hun" said the Girl who was standing in front of me with a smile on her face. It was not difficult for me to observe that whether the smile on anyone's face is natural or artificial. But I was not observing her smile and I didn't even have any reason for doing so. "Off course Yes, I don't have any private right over these chairs. Isn't it right?" I agreed and she sat next to me. She told me that she came to Court regarding her family matter. She was fighting for a divorce case against her husband but then after both husband and wife had decided to take divorce by mutual consent and on that day both have recorded statement in the Court and Court has passed the first motion divorce petition. She had to ask some queries about further procedure about second motion and about applying certified copies as she may have some trust deficit with her husband's advocate though I can't say anything about this with surety but yeah now I can observe that there is some kind of insecurity between advocates and clients specially in those cases wherein one counsel is appearing for both parties.

Although I didn't have law degree at that time but I was having some knowledge about the law and procedure about divorce cases, as I was dealing with them in my office. I shared the procedure and law with her as asked by her. And then she asked me that "Kya Har Din Itne Cases Lagte Hain Divorce Ke" and I could feel her pain when she asked me this. After the decision to stay with him for a lifetime after marriage, she was watching the relationship shatter. And she was my new stranger.

Maybe it is easy for an advocate to make drafting and file a case but it is difficult for the clients to deal with feelings, emotions, attachment and love. There is no doubt that it is their choice and their decision but part of me is aware that it is not easy for them to take a decision about separation. Sometimes it is in our hand to select our life partner and sometimes it is not in our hand to make choices. However, in both the cases, we used to believe that relationships are made in heaven and it is beyond our control. The question that is required to be answered is that why divorce cases are increasing and why it's becoming difficult for couples to maintain their marriage life and relationship.

She was young and confident Girl. Even though she was broken but she was independent and she was keen to start her fresh life. She shared her story with me. She was still in love with her husband but she was not ready to live with him. "Kya Wo Aapse Pyar Nahin Karta?" I asked her with curiosity. "Kya Pyaar Kafi Hai?" she immediately responded. "I don't Know, I am Single" I replied with a smile and she laughed at my response and I could observe that her laugh was natural and not artificial. "Uske Liye Aadmi Hone Ki Definition Kuch Aur Hai, Aur Mere Liye Muskil Hai Khud Ko Is Tarah Khote Huye Dekhna" she said. Thereafter I asked her that why she was not contesting case then she said that end of day we have to take decision and I took this decision to not to see his face and I don't want to remember the torture that he committed. She was in unbearable pain. I told her that I can imagine that it is difficult for you to take such decision when you are in love with someone but you have the right to disagree with your life partner and you have that freedom to take any independent decision. She said I am Strong but marriage and relationship made me weak.

She asked me that why man don't want to protect their relationship. She said that she tried her best to protect her marriage life but her husband was not happy with her mental, emotional and physical support. She said that she gave chances to him to improve. She wants to give respect to his love. "Keval Pyaar Aadmiyon Ke Liye Kafi Nahi Hai. Wo Shadi Karke Sochte Hain Jaise Koi Gudiya Unke Pass Hai Jisko Khilouna Banakar Roz Apne Hisab Se Khele". She was crying and further said that "Hum Bhi Insaan Hain, Hum Bhi Apni Zindagi Apne Hisab Se Zina Chahate Hain".

Every soul of this world is beautiful and all human beings are equal. Your life partner belongs to you and you have full rights over them, but this does not mean that you won't respect the rights of your life partner. We have to give respect to every soul. We are incomplete without our life partner. Love is not enough to be with someone. We have to understand them. We have to acknowledge their existence.

She told me that aggression is not the sole reason for divorce but that is the important reason and whenever she raised objection her husband used to beat her. "Har Baat Pe Ladai Hone Lagti Thi, Aakhir Kab Tak Aur Kis Had Tak Kisi Ki Demand Puri Kar Sakte Hain" she told me when I asked her about her response in resolving disputes before taking such step. "Hum Kab Tak Majburi Samajh Kar Sahate Rahenge, Kabhi na Kabhi to Kadam Lena Hi Hai" she said with courage. She taught me that someday we have to take a decision, and that to some strong decision.

It is not difficult for me to take stand on marital rape. This is the time when we have to make law regarding marital Rape and to recognize this issue. Don't be powerful and dominant just because of the fact that you are man. Those who are against marital rape are also having point that women can misuse this law because it is difficult to differentiate between rape and consented intercourse. But just because of the fear that someone can take advantage of law, we cannot give liberty to individuals to break the souls just because they are with them. For successful marriage, you need to have mutual understanding, adjustments, love and to give respect to your other half. We should think about mental and emotional support for a peaceful life.

Death Is Certain But Humanity Can Save A Life

"Helping hands don't ever disappoint you.

They can save you even from death."

Death is certain but sometimes we get an opportunity to save someone's life. There always comes a moment in our life where we have to take an instant decision whether to help the person who is in danger or just to leave him in that situation. Even if today we ignore a person in this kind of situation but what if tomorrow, we come across with the same situation. Don't you think at that point of time we would also need help like the person in need today.

My school days were fantastic. The only responsibility which we had during our school days was to do our homework and try to improve our grades. We didn't have any stress. All mates were having similar dress and there was no discussion about discrimination during school days. I am still missing those prayer times of my school. I have completed my schooling from Lodhi Road and at that time I used to reside at Khanpur, South Delhi. I had to take a bus for traveling. One day as usual, I took the bus from Lodhi Road after my school.

That day didn't seem to be unfortunate until and unless my bus had reached at Khanpur. When I stepped out of the bus door;

I didn't know what happened. The only thing I remember is that my leg was just under the tire of the bus and I was crying, then I lost my consciousness. When I came back I into my senses, I was in the bus and was in unbearable pain. Then I met with another two new strangers of my life. I saw a beautiful girl who was holding my hand and a boy who was standing next to her.

They took me from Khanpur to Batra Hospital where I was admitted to the Emergency ward. They informed my family and before my family reached there, the doctors had already started their work because both the Boy and Girl took the responsibility and fulfilled their duty as human. Later I came to know that my leg was fractured due to that accident.

In this world all are unknown to each other until and unless we have our first interaction. We all are strangers in this world, but then we came to know our relatives, the we made friends and some become our enemies. Then suddenly we realize that we have some obligations for all of them because we know about them. Yeah, at times we have also certain obligations against our enemies. But what about strangers? It is our choice to make our friends and enemies but we cannot forget about the fact that we all are humans. We all are having souls. We all have that opportunity to save someone or to help someone. As we are human beings we have certain duties or responsibilities towards all human beings and not only for those who are known to us.

They both were at Hospitals till night when my family decided to shift me from Batra Hospital to Max and I told both of them to go back to their home although they wanted to stay with me even in that Hospital.

During that accident, they had a choice to leave me there and they could have enjoyed the evening by forgetting about the accident and could have returned to their home safely. All strangers are used to do the same. We all have that tendency to forget everything or let me say ignore everything. We always want to avoid problems. We don't want to be in any tricky situation or else I can say that we all want to stay away from mess. We all have a certain kind of fear in our mind. But they were kind of different strangers.

When they had to take a decision, they took the decision to be with me and they taught me that it's not upon us to make relations but it's upon us to show our humanity when it is required. We always have to take decisions which are going to give a positive impact in someone else's life. If there is a situation of life and death, we should not wait for others reaction. We have to act as per the situations and circumstances.

When Hospitals Staffs were shifting me from emergency ward to Ambulance, that girl was with me and she told me that nothing is going to happen. She said that I will be able to walk again after a month, although it took 4 months for me to walk again. She realized that I was not feeling good after hearing about my fracture. Obviously, I was feeling terrible. At that time, I had many thoughts like maybe I will not be able to walk or maybe I am not going to join school for years or may be my leg is not going to recover and I would be in bed rest for the rest of my life. But When I was entangled between thoughts, that boy told me to have a glance at other corner side of the hospital where a man was urinating and that girl said with a laughter that "Kitna Besharm aadmi hai dekho to" and we all laughed which was essential at that moment to give a pause to my thoughts.

In real life situations we should not wait to give our reaction. We should give importance to the life of individuals. We have to feel the pain of others. We all are humans and we have to behave like humans.

Cause humanity is the best service which we all can do.

Response After Mistake Is Crucial

"Accepting your mistake makes you a thousand times better human than who commits one."

We all make mistakes in our life. Sometimes we do mistakes even after knowing the consequences and sometimes we are not aware that we are doing a mistake. Sometimes we intentionally commit mistake and sometimes without any malafide intentions we commit mistake. When we realize that we have made some mistake then Life gives chances to the person who committed mistake and to the person who was the sufferer.

After few days of accident, I was discharged from the ICU and I was doing well. Although the swelling of the leg was not over yet, but the pain was less now and doctors were saying that there was improvement in my health. It was difficult for me lying on the bed for such a long period of time but I didn't have any other option. I was compelled to be in such a situation. I could not complaint anything to anyone as I was taking breath even after such tragic and I was alive. Maybe the result of that accident could have been worse, but life gave me a second chance, which definitely gave some relief to my wounds.

"Ab Kaise Ho" heard the voice of man when I was lying on my bed. My eyes were closed and that voice was not familiar to me. I opened my eyes and replied by saying "filhaal to Zinda Hun" and then I laughed. But the man who was in front me was serious and he just smiled. I asked him who are you and he told me that he was the driver of that bus because of which I was in this condition. He was the new stranger of my life.

Sometimes it is difficult to understand that why we are in such difficult situation or condition in our life and then we try to find the reasons for that but sometimes it is difficult to find the reasons because sometimes we don't know that what actually happened and who is responsible for it. Even after knowing the fact that we are facing trouble because of one or two people, it is hard for someone to blame one person or to hold him responsible because by holding someone responsible, we are not going to achieve anything. We are not going to get anything by blaming someone for our position or situation or circumstances.

On that night of the horrible evening, that bus driver with his relative had reached at Hospital wherein I was admitted in ICU. Police officials also reached there for investigation. At that time the bus driver was under pressure because he was government employee and he was aware that now he was going to lose his job after complaint from our side. He tried to approach my family for financial aid but my family refused to accept the same. But when police officials have asked my family about the accident, they said that "our son told us that he was not sure that whether driver had committed any mistake or not and he told us to not to make any complaint against him as it might be possible that he has slipped." My family refused to make any complaint against Driver.

I believe that we cannot change our destiny and our luck is also not in our hand but we can improve our present and future with our deeds. We are none to blame someone else for our situation. That bus driver had the choice to leave me after accident at that place and he also had the option to not visit me after that night. When we decided not to complaint against him there, we had a choice to complaint against him and suspend him from his service or else to forget everything.

Bus Driver was crying when he was standing in front of me and I asked him why he is crying, he told me that you saved me and my family because without this job I was not in position to teach my children and to give anything to my family. I held his hand and told him that "but that's nothing in front of what you've done". Some part of me was saying that it may be possible that at the time of accident if Bus Driver had not put the brakes of the bus at the right time and didn't turn the tier back, my leg would be crushed and I could not walk for the rest of my life. I told him that "Sahab Aapne to Meri Zindagi Bachai Hai" and asked him "Bus Kahan Hai" and he told me that "Bahar Khadi Hai". I told him to not to take any tension and to do work.

He taught me that making mistake is not easy. Realization of mistake is important. I am not sure that if he had made any mistake or not. Even if you hit someone don't leave anyone in that terrible painful condition.

Show some humanity as shown by my stranger.

Be Happy With Whatever You Have

"Baggage of responsibility does not care about your age or status; it comes to the person who is capable of handling it."

Sometimes we feel that we are surrounded by problems, circumstances and compulsion and somehow, we think that we are in position wherein we don't have any other option. We think that we don't have any reason to be happy. We ask question that why god is doing this with us. We want someone to be blamed. We have a perception that only we have problems in our life and other individual are in better situation. We think that life is tough for us. Whether we are right or whether we are just trying to satisfy ourselves by giving excuses.

I must say that it was risky to decide whether to visit Bodh Gaya on the day of Holi Or not. Celebration of Holi in Bihar is special but only for those who want to play Holi with people of Bihar. I am not pointing out on them. They are special and we cannot judge them only on the basis of some energetic youth. We wanted to visit Bodh Gaya therefore after Visiting Mohabodhi Temple, we were looking for E-Rickshaw and one boy without colour in his face came to us and said "Aao Har

Mandir Ghumate Hain Hum Aapko". Then we asked him that why he is not playing Holi and he replied "Abhi Bahut Time Hai, Pahale Kaam Karna Hai Aapko Ghumana Hai". We decided to go with him and he was my new stranger.

We have a tendency to complain about life but I don't think that we take a pause to think that what we will get after making complaints. It is difficult to be happy with whatever we have and may be that will restrict our improvement but we should be thankful for our present condition.

After 10 minutes we got that opportunity to see the celebration of Holi on the Road of Bodh Gaya and we were forced to return to the same place from where we took E-Rickshaw. My stranger tried his best and waited for 10-15 minutes at the corner of road but Youths of Bodh Gaya were not ready to stop their celebrations. It was his first ride in the morning but we didn't have any other alternative other than leaving him and walk to the other side of road.

"Are Tum Phir Mil Gaye" I told him after I found him at the time of leaving from hotel in Bodh Gaya to go to Gaya Railway

Station. We had our return ticket on that Day itself and we were stressed that whether we will get any transportation or not. Fortunately, I found him and for the first time I found my stranger for the second time on the same day. "Kya E-Rickshaw Ja Payega Station Tak" I asked him as I was not sure. "Kyo Nahi Jayega Aap Log Jaha Jayenge Wahi Jayega".

He was very young and impressive mind of Bodh Gaya. He stopped his E-Rickshaw at one place. He told us that he was building his house over there. I could see that he was asking questions with masons about developments and work. I could listen the sound of responsibility in his voice. He was handling and managing his family and all expenses. He was 24-year-old young boy. "Padhai Kyo Nahi Ki" I asked him with curiosity and he replied with smile by saying that "Padhai Karne Ka Sochne ka Time Nahi Tha, Ghar Sambhalna Tha". "Ab Ghar Sambhal Raha Hun, E-Rikhshwa Ki Shop Hai, Bahut E-Rickshaw Hai Mere Pass, Bahut Log Mujhe Jante Hain, Ladke Kaam Karr he Hai Mere Under" he told me and he was saying this from his heart and I could feel the same. He stopped at his shop and took new E-Rikshaw with full charge.

We all have regrets in our life except and some exceptions too. 24-year-old young boy who is driving his E-Rickshaw without thinking about his dreams, his past and his future. He was responsible. He was managing his family at the time when he should be at College for his Higher Study. He didn't have any regrets that he didn't get the opportunity to study. He accepted the challenge of Life and he was fighting with strength and confidence. He was able to do everything because he accepted the challenge given by life. He didn't waste his time and energy just by blaming upon others and thinking about problems of his life. He could have sat at home and could have approach the easiest way to live life by taking wrong routes but he had chosen to do hard work.

When we reached Station, another E-Rickshaw driver came to us and told us that you got a very good driver, he is very hard working. I also didn't have any reason to disagree with him. I asked his name but I am not disclosing herein. Till evening he was not having any colour on his face but he had filled his life with beautiful colors. Colors that could not be separated.

What Is The Real Purpose Of Life

"Don't chase life, live it, most importantly love it."

We all are chasing something in our life. We all have desires, objectives and expectations in our life. We are not satisfied with whatever we have and wherever we are. We want to improve our current situation which is good for living a life. We must have some motivation to live life. We are living in this era where competition is tough and it is difficult for us to sustain and it is much more difficult to be successful. Even after living a peaceful life Or even after fulfilling our current goals and expectations, we can't say with surety that we will live a satisfactory life.

Gaya is a beautiful City and Bodh Gaya is among one of the most peaceful places of this Country. During Holi Vacations I was in Bodh Gaya to visit Mahabodhi Temple and Gaya City. We all are searching different way for motivation, meditation and yoga but we are not giving importance to our history and our great leaders. We are reading different books but we are not ready to read our scriptures.

Whole country was celebrating festival of color Holi on that Day. Most of the shops were closed but somehow, I found one tea shop just opposite of Bodhi Temple. I found one monk sitting there at the tea shop. I could observe that he was a peaceful and a satisfactory soul. I asked him "where are you from?" and he told me that he is from Darjeeling. His voice was harmonious. I decided to sit with him and interact with him. I met with my new stranger of my life.

After visiting Mahabodhi, a great awakening temple and Bodhi tree under which Lord Buddha gained enlightenment, I got some different and exceptional experience. In this world where everyone is busy in their life, I saw people there who were doing meditation and yoga. One can observe that they are free from the artificial world. If you ask anything to them, they will give reply to you with a smile. You cannot observe any irritation or frustration on their faces. They are free from anger, jealousy and ego. That scene from that place wherein everyone was doing meditation, sitting at different areas of Bodhi Temple and reciting mantras was unique and memorable.

"Money is important but not every time" he said this with lots of expressions in his face. I asked him that is it possible to remain in peace without being a monk because it is not possible for everyone to leave everything. He didn't take time to reply and told me that "Yes, but it will take time to understand this fact". I was curious and when a person is curious then the person will have lots of question in his mind. I asked him "Why?". Then the person in Attractive Yellow Dress replied "Because people are chasing something without knowing the objective of life and when they feel tired then they will automatically choose the path of meditation and peace because that is the only way of living peaceful and satisfactory life".

Are we aware about the objective of our life? Why are we living a life? What is the definition of life, peaceful life and satisfactory life for us? There is no doubt about the fact that we all are chasing something without knowing that what we want from our life. Money is not an ultimate goal. Having status in society is not enough. No one can say that these all are not relevant but sometimes we have to ask ourselves that after getting all materialistic things whether we can say that we are living peaceful life and whether we are satisfied with our life or not.

"Everyone is pretending that they are living happy life but their faces are telling some different story. They don't have time to spend some time with their family" he was saying with a flow and at that time I didn't have any intentions to interrupt him. "People are lonely even after having everything". "And because of that they are not having satisfactory and peaceful life." I could not help myself and completed his sentence. "Absolutely" he was happy with my interruption and I could observe that from his reaction. He further added "People are aware that life is beyond materialistic things but they are not ready to understand this".

We cannot say anything with surety about another life after death. We have this beautiful life. We should not waste this beautiful gift of god only by living life by closing our eyes and soul. We have this opportunity to promote peace, love and humanity. We should search beauty of life rather than chasing something. We have to be grateful with whatever we have and we should be happy for having such a beautiful life.

45

Are We Changing The Meaning Of Love ?

"Above Love and Lust, Respect and Understanding comes first."

Human Touch is important to feel someone else's presence. Especially when we are living in the era of Corona Virus, we can feel the importance of Touch as we all are making 6ft. Distance with other individual. We all want to be loved and we all want mental, physical and emotional support. Life is incomplete without Love. We want to be with our life partner at every place and every moment we want to love our life partner. But at that special moment are we creating uncomfortable situations for Someone? Whether we are taking liberty of Privacy by showing love in Public?

"Agla Station Chandni Chowk Hai" heard announcement after taking metro from Kashmiri Gate after my office. Fortunately, I got a seat on that Day. Believe me it is not easy to get seat from Kashmiri Gate. One old Dadi wearing red saree was standing in front of me. I vacated the seat for her. Initially she refused to take by saying that you are not sitting at Ladies Seat. After then she accepted my request and took the seat. She thanked me and I just smiled. She was my new stranger.

After sometime I noticed that she was saying something to the couples who were sitting in the front row of her. Although I was physically there but my mind was not there. I was lost as usual. But that discussion between couple and Dadi ji compelled me to take notice of that. "Aapko Kya Fark Padta Hai" heard voice of a Girl who was sitting with a Boy and Dadi Ji was telling her that "Mujhe to Kya Fark Padega Maine to Duniya Lekh Li Beti. I was not aware about the origin of debate but from the age and color of her hair, I agreed with Dadi's Words. I told Dadi Ji "Chhodiye Aap Kyo Apna Mood Kharab Kar Rahi Hain" then she said "Mujhe to Bus in Logon Ki Fikr Hoti Hai Bete".

She said that kissing and touching body parts is not love. She told me that "Ye to Bachhe Hain Inko Kya Malum Pyaar Kise Khate Hain". "To Phir Aap hi Bataye Pyaar Kya Hai" I laughed. She told me that it is not easy for them to see couples while doing such stuff in public and it is uncomfortable for them to see such youths. "Pyaar to Hum Bhi Karte The,

Chhittiyan Likh Likh Kar Sath Hone Ka Anubhav Karte The. Pyaar Dikhawa Jyada Ho Gaya Hai Aur Sadko par Baithke Yahi Sab Karna Pyaar Ho Gaya Aajkl".

We cannot blame anyone and even I am not blaming those couple. No one can blame anyone. Everyone is having their own definition of Love. Having said that we have to seriously think about our approach. May be what is right and appropriate for us is not right and appropriate for others. We don't have to change the way of are living or loving but we also have to listen other's view. We just cannot deny everything by saying that you will not understand due to generation gap or by saying that don't be jealous. Maybe we are taking it in a wrong direction without knowing that where we want to reach.

"Ye Humari Privacy Hai, Iska Adhikaar Hai Hume, Aap Kyo Hume Suna Rahi Ho" once again girl took her stand but I didn't like her tone and the way she spoke with Dadi. Maybe she was not happy with the way Dadi was getting attention from other people but having said that the girl had made mistake while making her point. As a Law Student and being in this legal profession I was having knowledge of law and right of privacy but that was not the only reason for jumping in that argument. I was feeling hurt with the way the girl was responding. I had to take stand for Dadi Ji. "Privacy ka Matlb Ye Nahi Hai Ki Aap Log Kuch Bhi Kare aur Umar Dekh Kar Bolna Sikhiye, Ho Sakta Hai Aap Log Galat Na Ho lekin Ye Tarika to Nahi Baat Karne Ka" Although I was not interested but I made my point and neither the girl nor the boy said anything and I was happy that they understood my point.

Right to Privacy is fundamental right of every Citizen but you cannot claim that right by doing any act in public places. Let's not talk about rights and law. Morally we have to think that is it right to do so called romantic acts in metro stations, stairs, market or any other public places. Believe me it is uncomfortable for youth also to face such situations whenever they are with their family. Don't restrict love to only physical touch. No one will get anything by showing their love and feelings in public. Maybe I am sounding like I am orthodox or am not from 21st century but I have to promote message of Dadi Ji.

Dadi Ji shared her life experience and her Love life with me. She told me that life was more beautiful during her old days and People were more romantic during those days. She said that today's generation has failed to understand Love and romance and therefore they are living an unhappy and unsatisfactory life. Let's Try to Understand Love and romance before loving someone.

How To Make A Perception ?

"Your small acts have great impact."

Experience plays an important role in our life. We usually make our own perceptions and assumptions based on our past experience. We think about our experience before taking any decisions. Different people from different places give us experience about them and about their place. But it's upon us to either make someone's experience better or help them to have a better perception and assumption about us and our place.

As a Law Student, for me participating in Moot Court Competition was most interesting and a challenging part of my college life. Though Participating in College was also competitive but going outside the College for National Competition was different and special experience. I with my other 2 participants and one brother of participant went to Bangalore for National Moot Court Competition. I got different experience from south. Although North India is sharing different culture and customs with South India but having said that I found that people from South are humbler and more innocent.

We were there for three days and on third day at 12:00 Noon, we had to check out from the hotel. We had decided to see beautiful city on third day. We told the man at the counter of Hotel that we are going to visit the city so you can give room to anyone who will come as we are not using the room. He agreed with us. But in evening when we have reached at Hotel he asked for charges for a Day. We tried to make our point but he was not ready to understand that and as we had to the take flight, we didn't have time to waste so we decided to give money to him as per his demand. We were at Ground floor of the Hotel and we all were discussing about the incident. May be somewhere we also had committed mistake but we believed in the words and we didn't have any reason for not doing so. We all were surprised with the way the person reacted especially after meeting with some beautiful souls in that city. "Itna Acha Trip Tha, Bus Is Aadmi ke Chakkar mein Mind Upset Ho Gaya" one of us was making her point. "Asa Kya Huwa?" an old person with white hair ,who was sitting on the main chair interrupted. And he was my new stranger.

Small Acts are underrated but those acts and efforts are important. They can provide some relief to someone. They can be the reason of happiness in someone's life. We are trying to ignore or avoid such acts and we are not giving importance to them but by doing one small act you can give happiness to other. Especially when you are in such a position to take decision or to put some efforts then you will have to do whatever you can or whatever is in your hand.

"Kuch Nahi Bus Upar Wale Hotel Ne" I was saying but before completing my sentence, he told me that "Kya Kiya Usne?" I explained everything to him and my other partners also made their point. He was very upset after listening to our story. He sent one boy to call the man who was in upper floor. He told him that "I can listen anything about my hotel but I can't tolerate anything about my city. Don't take anything from them. They are not liable to give any money as they did not use room and they informed you about their plan." He scolded him and he directed him to return our money. As per his direction the man returned our money.

Till that evening we were having great experience from that city before that incident and even after that incident we forgot about the same and were not having any grudge about city only because of one incident but I was surprised by the way the person said that I will not tolerate anything against my city. He was thinking that we were leaving city with a bad experience. Later we came to know that he was the head of that premises and hotel person was doing his business under that man. He was a tenant in that premises. He has the option to remain silent but he chooses to speak for his city and for his place. He was aware that we don't have any financial issue even though he took up this issue and directed the hotel's person to return our money just because he did not want that we leave that city by creating any bad perception about our trip.

We all have that duty to make a person feel better of another place. We should give respect to them. By our behaviour, people will make their perception and we all have that opportunity to assist them in making good experience and perception.

Religion Is All About Teaching And Preaching

"Understand the True meaning of Religion and Be a Human and Promote Humanity."

It is beyond our control that in which family we are born and it is not in our hand to decide our religion as we adopt our religion by birth. We follow our religious duties inspired from our parents and relatives. Children will learn from their parents and from whatever they will tell them about their religion. We read scriptures of our religion from our home. We read about our culture, history and faith and we follow our custom. What we are following and how we are doing our religious ceremonies is our private matter. But whether we are becoming hardcore about one particular religion and whether we are properly understanding the message of our religious books or not and can we learn from other religion's religious books? By not following or not reading and understanding about other's religion book, do we have any right to make any comments? We are limiting ourselves by not expanding our knowledge and information about other religion.

Gorakhdham Temple is one of the attractions of Gorakhpur and I planned to visit the temple so I took a bus from Anand Vihar to Gorakhpur. Travelling in Bus during nights is also a different experience. Lights were closed as all the passengers were sleeping but my eyes were not ready to close. I was trying to see outside of window by removing curtails. Two passengers who were sitting in the seats equal to my seat were singing some song. I was not being able to understand the lyrics but their voice was euphonious. "Gorakhpur Kitna Dur Hai" a boy who was not comfortable in speaking Hindi asked me and I told him that it will take some time so you can sleep but he told me that they are remembering God. Then I enquired about the song and the girl told me that they are singing night's prayer. They both are Christian from Kerala and my new strangers.

I am Hindu by religion and I read and watch about my religious History Culture. And I don't get the opportunity to read Kuran or Bible or any other religious books of other religion but I read some part of Kuran during Triple Talaq Controversy and some part of bible during Christmas. But I was not aware about them in details. Part of me is telling me that all religious books were promoting same message but part of me is directing me to read about them. It is not possible to get information and knowledge without reading about them. I failed to find any reason to not to read about other religion's religious books. Nowadays we all are commenting about other religion without having any knowledge about them. We all are humans and we can make mistakes but no religion is telling us to make mistakes. Individual can follow his religion in a wrong way but we cannot blame entire religion for that mistake of any individual.

During that night when most of the passengers were sleeping, we three decided to debate and discuss about our religion. Girl had started that conversation with beautiful example. She told me that if you are in swimming pool and you don't know how to swim then what will happen? I told her that I will try to save myself. Then she asked me that how because you don't know how to swim. She told me that you need someone who can save you. I agreed. She said that then God will come to save you. She added upon that god is telling us to be courageous and strong. He will never leave you. She said that whenever you are in such situation and you will remember him from your soul, God will come to save you.

I told her that we also believe in same manner. If we are facing some difficult situation then we think about god and we have the belief that he will come to save us. Then the boy gave another example about Forbidden fruit. He told me that Adam and Eve ate an apple from the forbidden tree in the Garden. Forbidden Fruit is a name given to the fruit growing in the Garden which God commands mankind not to eat. But Adam and Eve ate the fruits from the tree of Knowledge of Good and Evil which is forbidden by God. He told me that it is difficult for Human to follow good deeds because we are attracting towards forbidden Acts which are illegal and immoral.

We want to do experiments in our life. We want to do such acts which are not permitted by our parents or our society. We think that we are under boundation or they are trying to limit us. We think that they are controlling our freedom. We think that they are not permitting us to see the world but we neither have time to think that restriction is good for us or not.

That night was full of wisdom and knowledge for me as I was getting knowledge about other's religion and at the same time, I was sharing stories about my religion. Sometimes we don't agree with each other but I have to say that all three were good listeners and they have that beautiful skill to share their views with illustrations.

"As we are discussing in such healthy environment, I want to understand about one controversial issue?" now I want to understand from them about this controversial issue as I heard about it from others but I never got that opportunity to hear from Christians. "Yes, Yes Please" they both agreed and I raised issue regarding conversion. I asked them to tell me about their views about conversion. I asked them that Is it good or moral to convert people from one religion to another by giving some money. Is it possible that the people who are getting money will follow religion after conversion?

"Why people are only blaming for giving money? Why they are not blaming for them who are taking money because by giving money we are providing help to poor" though I know it was hard question but they didn't show any kind of irritation or frustration after my question and a boy responded. "But you can help them without telling them about conversion?" "Yes, we are helping people but unfortunately some people are doing this conversion activity which is wrong and immoral." Girl gave instant reply to my question.

They told me that you cannot tell people to follow some particular religion. They have that right to choose but if anyone will come and say that I want to follow Christianity then we are not going to say no because it is our responsibility to share wisdom and knowledge. I don't have any reason to disagree with them. If people are willing to change their religion then that is their choice and that is their right. They also agreed with me that conversion by giving money is not a good act. They told me that this is not permissible but some people are doing and defaming their religion. It is okay to understand about other's religion. You can learn lessons from their scriptures. What I understand is all religions are promoting and giving the message of peace, love and humanity and we can learn from all of them.

65

Riots: Killing Humanity From Our Society

"Riots end up with rivers of blood while peace demands no shred of blood."

2020 is not the good year for Delhi. Students from JNU were protesting against fee hikes which became violent and then CAA controversy, open firing, Police versus students issue in Jamia, police versus advocates issues and then Riots. No one was in position to think about humanity before religion during riots. 2-3 days were difficult, dangerous and unimaginable for the people of Delhi. After riots we got information about loss, loss which was unbearable for Hindus as well as for Muslims and no one was in position to explain that what people from either religion got from that violence. Why we are becoming violent and why we are attracted towards hatred than peace? Why people who are following their respective religion are influenced by hatred?

It was difficult for me to go out during riots but after 2 days I had to go to High Court and I booked my Taxi. It is not relevant to take the name of the company. I felt peace after storm in the air of the city. "Kya Baat Hai, Hawa Phir se Kharab Lag Rahi Hai" I have to admit that it is difficult for me to sit and travel without saying anything. "Kharab Kyo Nahi Hogi Itni Aag Jo Lag Rahi Hai" I can feel the painful and hopeless sound of my taxi driver and he is my new stranger and he was Muslim. It is not possible to talk about riots without mentioning about religion.

He told me that he was facing difficult situation and it is not easy to survive during riots. "1947 se Lad Rahe Hai Sahab Ye Log, Aakhir Mila Kya?" he asked me and I opened the window of the car and thought about his question. I know that he was upset with whatever was happening during those days. "Hume Sabit Karna Muskil Ho Jata Hai ki Hume Hinduon se Koi Samasya Nahi Hai". I told him that "Bhid Mein Kaun Hindu Kaun Muslim Janab Wo to Sabko Maarne Lagte Hain" but he was not agreeing with me. "Log Chun Chun Ke Maarte Hain Sir, Kiska Ghar Kaun Sa Hain Aur Kiski Dukaan Kaun Si Hai Pata Karne Ke Baad Jalate Hain". Though he was absolutely right because I heard that in news bulletin but part of me was not allowing me to believe that fact. "Bhid Ke Pass Waqt Kaha

Hota Hai Sochne Ka" I tried to justify my point though I have many reasons to believe his statement.

Blood is red of everyone but unfortunately, we realized this fact after seeing blood stains in roads and streets. We do not see this when we shed each other's blood in the riots. Government will calculate and assess lost and announce compensation. Police will try to investigate and arrest 2 or 3 persons after riots and media will sensationalize the whole issue in a dramatic way and then people will forget everything. That is how we are learning to live after every riot.

"Hindu Ho Ya Muslim Log to Mar Rahe Hai, Ghar Aur Dukanee to Jal Rahe Hain Kisko Kya Fayda Hoga?" he was saying with broken heart and I didn't have any words to compensate him. "Mere Bhai Ki Redi Thi Sir Jala Diya Raat Ko Aakaar Kuch Bhi Nahi Bacha" he was the brother of Victim and I can understand his pain. "Mein Hi Kyon Hindu Bhaiyon Ke Bhi Dukanee Jala Diye Sab Rakh Ho Gaya Sir In

Logon Ki Galti Kya Hai Ye to Bus Apna Kaam Kar Rahe The."

It is difficult to compensate any victim after loss of any family member or loss of their property. It is easy for us to see all these stuffs on news but after losing their livelihood and family they don't have anything in their life. Rioters had snatched everything from them i.e. their family, their earnings and their happiness. What will we get after knowing the religion of rioters or the religion of Victim after such terrible incident and loss?

He told me that whether they were Hindus or Muslims, are they not humans. They don't have any emotions and they just want to break our community by creating this kind of situation and by violence. "Kuch Logon Ki Vajah se Hum Badnaam Ho Rahe Hain, Hume Kaha Jata Hai Tum Pakistani Ho. Hum to Is Desh Ko Apna Sab Kuch Maante Hai Sir Phir Bhi Humse Hi Sabut Mannge Jate Hain.Humare Purvajon Ne to Yahan Rahane Ka Faisla Kiya Tha. Maybe he had a feeling that some people are not accepting them or they are not tolerating them. "Koi Kuch Kaha Deta Hai to Phir Sab Muslimon Ko Shak Ke Najron Se Dekhte Hain". On that Day I didn't explain or elaborate anything to him. I just heard him because he was in pain but we have to understand that Religion was, is, and will unite us but for that unity we have to understand our religion and we have to be human. Violence is not a solution and we didn't and will not get anything from riots.

For Kashmir, Education Is The Only Effective Weapon

"Give them Books, they will use this weapon for development."

Education is important for everyone. Every child has the right to get education. Because of this education we are able to understand what is right and what is wrong for us. We have that ability to think about our future, our aim and our purpose of life after getting education. If we are not giving the opportunity to get education then we are not only restricting growth of any individual but also, we are giving other elements to take advantage of innocent youth. There is a difference between not having resources for getting education and not be able to take proper classes. We always have to understand the difference between compulsion and choice.

I was about to take flight for the first time and then I was about to Visit Heaven of this Earth i.e. Kashmir with my family. I was curious and excited for both. Kashmiri's are beautiful. They are natural and energetic. We took flight from Delhi to Kashmir and after arrival at Srinagar Airport, we had booked one small bus for our trip as we were in group. One boy was there who was helping the bus driver. He told us "Hum

Ghumayega Aapko Kashmir Aapko Bahut Mazza Aayega".
Innocent and Straightforward boy from Kashmir was ready to
roam with us who was about to help us to see beautiful heaven.
He was my new stranger.

Education is also a weapon and individual can use the same for
making change. We cannot totally leave everything for a
student getting education. Recruitment of teachers and
opening building is not enough for providing education,
especially in Kashmir. Rights are different and duty and
responsibility is different and we have to understand the
difference. It is important to observe that whether every
student is getting quality education after admission in school
or they are getting degree after passing exams without proper
classes.

"Humara to 6 Mahine Kisi Na Kisi Vajah Se School Band
Rahate Hai" disappointed young boy answered when I asked
question about his school and education and classes in

Kashmir during winters. I can imagine his pain and his compulsion from the tone of his voice.

"Kabhi Curfew Lag Jata Hai Kabhi Itni Barf Padti Hai" he was sharing his experience and I didn't have any intention to interrupt him. "Jam Jate Hai Pure Pani Barf Ho Jata Hai Raat Ka Rakha Huwa". "Humare Liye Possible Nahi Hai Ase Mein Class Jana School Bhi Band Ho Jate Hai". He was not happy with that but he was aware that no one can do anything about this natural process. We can't blame anyone for that. "Lekin Isme Kar Bhi Kya Sakte Hai?" I asked him. "Isme Agar Kuch Nahi Kar Sakte to Jo Itna Politics Ki Vajah Se Band Hota Hai Usko to Rok Sakte Hai" he was upset and frustrated with the system.

We discussed about the situation in Kashmir and heard about that in Television. Media persons called other's Nation people in evening debate and entertained us. We do not understand and realize the seriousness of the subject. For us, it is just news about curfew but only those who are residing and living in

Kashmir can understand that what is the impact, how it affects and result of this kind of situation. Those students who are not being able to attend school and those who are unable to read all chapters of all subjects can understand the loss. We cannot imagine the mental stress of the school going students.

"Aap Hi Batao Hum Pass Ho Bhi Jate Hai Exam Mein Lekin Humara Syllabus to Pura Nahi Ho Pata Kabhi" he was telling about his classes. "Kabhi Pure Saal Lagataar Class Ho Hi Nahi Pati Jab Hume Knowledge Hi Puri Nahi Ho Payegi to Hum Kaise Compete Kar Payenge Bankiyo Se" he had a valid point and I agreed with him. "Kehte Hai Kashmiri Yuva Asa Hai Waisa Hai Bhatak Gaya Hai Humari Badnami Hoti Hai" I was just listening. "Agar Humari Classes Aur Padhai Lagatar Ho to Sab Apni Apni Padhai Mein Busy Hote Hum to Sab Desh Ke Liye Kuch Karna Chahate Hai Lekin Ase Curfuew Lagta Rahega Aur Aadhe Time Barf Padti Rahegi to Humara Kaise Hoga Growth". He asked some valid question.

At the time when we are talking about online classes during pandemic, Indian Government should and will have to think about online classes in Kashmir especially during winters and during the time of curfew so that students can take proper education without any interruption.

Phone: Our Need Or Our Addiction

"An inevitable gadget invented for betterment but now leading towards our degradation."

Phones are important for everyone. We don't need newspaper to read and we don't require television to watch. We are having friends and family in our phone. I may say that we are having everything in our phone. It is difficult for us to survive without phones in today's era. If I will use 'addiction' then it may sound negative so I am using 'need' so that we can satisfy ourselves by saying that we are just fulfilling our need by using phones and we cannot live without our phone. I don't find any demerits of using phone as we have to be updated and active. We can interact with anyone in the world and we can use our phone during urgency. But when we are using phones, are we ignoring those who are physically present with us or are we forgetting to make connection with souls.

After a tired day I was in the metro and I was thinking about my day. I didn't get a seat but I was also not alone. It is very exciting experience to see that every individual standing in metro looking for the person who is about to vacate the seat so that they could grab that seat. One Sardar Ji was looking for seat and when one seat was vacant in front of him then one young boy who had plugged in earphones overtook Sardar Ji and took the seat. We both passed smile at each other but neither he nor me said anything to that boy. Sardar Ji was senior and i could assume that from his beard. Thereafter, I asked another man to give his seat to Sardar Ji and I was happy to see that he gave that seat to him. Sardar Ji got a seat and said thank you to that boy and me. After some minutes I got a seat next to him. He was my new stranger.

"Aap Phone Nahi Chala Rahe?" old man with his powerful voice asked me and it was strange for me to hear that question. "Ji?" I asked him instead of replying his question as I was needed some more explanation to understand what he was trying to say. "Nahi Samne Aapas Aur Khade Huye Logo Ko Dekhiye Sabke Pass Hatho Mein Phone Hai Lekin Aap Nahi Chala Rahe". "Bus Mein Logo Ke Chahare Dekh Raha Hun, Har Chahara Ek Alag Kahani Batati Hai". I told him and he said "Absolutely, but nowadays who really does have time for all this?" He was not happy with the way people were using phone and coincidently majority were using mobile over there.

Life is definitely boring and incomplete without our phones but at some point, of time we have to think that what is the limit of using phone and how we should use our phone without disturbing our normal behaviour. Some other day we have to realize that phone is our need and not our addiction and we have to learn that we are becoming more addicted to our phone rather than using the same for some purpose.

"Aaj Kal Ke Logon Se Jyda Busy Huwa Karte The Hum, Tab Bhi Itne Busy Dikhte Nahi The Jitne Aaj Kal Ke Log Dikhte Hain" he pointed his finger towards the phone users as he said this. He is basically complaining about them but I refused to entertain his complaint. "Busy to Nahi Lekin Din Bhar Kaam Karke Entertain Kar Rahe Honge Khud Ko" I tried to make point on behalf of them. "Agar Ye Entertainment Ke Liye Hai to Phir Aaj Kal Kuch Aur Ho Hi Nahi Raha" we both laughed at his statement. "Hum Apne Zamane Mein Apne 2-3 Dosto Ke Sath Khush Rahate The, Aaj Kal Logon Ke Hazaron Dost Hai, Sab Kuch Phone Se Hi Chal Raha Hai. Connection to

Nahi Ho Pata, Srif Phone Par Hi Sari Duniya Chal Rahi Hai".

He further said that "Na Kisi Ko Metro Ke Gate Khulne Ka

Pata Chal Raha Hai, Na Stairs Ka Pata Chal Raha Hai aur Na

Ghar Mein Sath Baithe Logon Ka Pata Hai" although I also

used phone and I think some time more than the "Normal

Limit" but I agreed with him.

Phone is necessary but not everytime. Those thousands

artificial friends are irrelevant if we lose connection with those

who are with us. We have to fix time for using phone and we

have to understand that indirectly we are reducing the

importance of human connection and human touch while

using phone when we are sitting with someone or sitting with

our family.

"Logon Ke Pass Itna Kuch Hai Kahane Ko, Samajhne Ko

Lekin Kisi Ke Pass Waqt Hi Nahi Hai" as he said this, he

meant that people are busy with phone even at the time of

consuming meal. He said that they are not ready to sit without

using phone and this is causing mental illness for many of us.

I have to say that life is more beautiful without phones and we just have to understand and realize that point. Next time think before using your phone while sitting with your family and while taking your meal.

There's always a limit for everything and same goes for phones.

Our real world matters more than the virtual world.

83

Right Time For Spiritual Path

"In this virtual artificial world, spiritual values matter
the most."

While I was coming back to Delhi, I took bus from Gorakhpur and for me, travelling in bus is a different experience. "Khidki to Khol Lijiye" I heard the passionate voice from one young and attractive youth who further told me "Upper wala button to khol sakte hain". It is my habit to close top button of my shirt and usually I prefer to wear in that manner. I convey my preference to him and he understood the same. I was reading one book and that boy who was sitting one seat back from my seat again told me that "may I sit with you". I agreed and he became my new stranger.

It is unique and special experience for me to have conversation with strangers. He was new for me but after interacting with him I felt that I was having long old relation with this guy. It is our perception that we can make relationship and we can feel the connection after making relations but I believe that it's not upon us to feel in a particular way for someone and it's not upon us to create connections. It's all about time when you meet with someone and you feel that we are having different connections.

He was, and I hope he still is, great worshipper of Lord Shiva and more than that he was doing meditation and concentration practice. He was about 17 years old young boy who was talking about importance of mediation and yoga. We discussed about life, objectives of life and about why we are giving importance to material things than spiritual life.

"Bhaiya Iski Koi Age Nahi Ho Sakti" he told me when I asked about his age. His maturity at this age is incredible and unimaginable. "Mein Subha 4 Baje Uthkar Shiv Ki Bhakti Karta Hun aur Dhyaan Karta Hun Aur Jo Shanti Isse Milti Hai Bhaiya Mein Bata Nahi Sakta". His energy level was in different level when he was sharing his experience with me.

He was younger than me but when I got that opportunity to interact with him, I learnt that how much energy we have with our personality and how much we can utilize that energy in our life. Every individual is different but after meeting with him, I understand that it's not about age and it's not about right time however it's all about your intent to do something. The way might be different for everyone but realizing the importance of spirituality is more important to live peacefully. He taught me that we may choose our own path for meditation but it's important to show our right intent for utilizing overall energy of our body so that we can manage our life in appropriate and effective way.

Suhail: Today's Inspiring Youth

"Youths are the future; they are seed for the plant of change."

Another beautiful conversation with one Kashmiri Youth who was inspiring and encouraging youths of Kashmir. Sharing this conversation to understand and realize that age is just a number and you can bring change if you are willing to do the same.

"I want to bring smiles on the faces of people, each face inspiring me to go further to make more people smile," said Suhail Mehraj, a youth activist who represented Kashmir at UN Youth Assembly. Suhail is also one of the advisers in the UNDP board.

Suhail, who works with different volunteer initiatives for the welfare of the people in Kashmir, believes in living a resourceful life and aims on educating people on their rights and social responsibilities. He wants to change the perception about Kashmiri youth and improve the education system in the valley.

Raaz Dheeraj Sharma: How do you see yourself different from other youths of valley?

SM: I don't think that I'm different. I was brought up here in the valley only, and I performed every sort of activity here only. I am just performing my duty.

RDS: Tell us about your education awareness program ? When did you think or made your mind that you want to do something to improve education scenario in the valley?

SM: I was 16 when I along with my schoolmates decided to work to improve the education situation in Kashmir. What inspired me was that I wanted Kashmir to be a profound learning space that has a good share in the global development. During my conversations with students, I found that learning level was very pathetic. A lot of children couldn't go to school due to many reasons like lack of financial recourses, motivation, etc. Many were the first-generation learners. After witnessing all this, I could not sleep properly. My mind was full of questions like how we will become a developed society if we are unable to educate children properly. I started two-day

(Saturday and Sunday) teaching program in a week in my district, selecting areas where education was yet a new thing. I motivated people to educate their children. I made them realize the importance of education and how it could be used as a tool to bring positive changes in Kashmir and also help them voice their issues. Finally, I got some 250 students of different age group enrolled in my initiative. Some of them were not able to read and write, but within four months the efforts showed results. They were able to read and write. After that, I got about some 45 school dropouts back in school. Last year, I started a campaign to motivate students who had the privilege to be in schools' colleges and universities, to help in bringing Kashmir close to the progress, by initiating different initiatives.

RDS: You are also working with UN. Tell us something about that?

SM: I work with different organs of UN, such as UNDP, UNICEF and ILO as their young advisory member for their various projects in Asia and West Africa. Helping them in forming the ground policies and strategies to meet the goals. Apart from that, I'm also assisting the youth and policymakers of Nigeria for making a difference, advising them on certain issues like Education & Health.

RDS: You delivered one speech at UN Youth Assembly on how to enhance education in developing nations. Tell us something about that and share your experience with us.

SM: In February, I got an opportunity to speak in one of the world's prestigious podium General Assembly as a part of Youth Assembly. I shared views about the initiatives that I started in my state and how I used education as a key for reformation. I stressed upon the fact that there's huge young population in the world and that youth should take the responsibility to shape the future of world that is full of positivity and possibilities. We can't have a good future until we collaborate. If someone is suffering in America or any other place of the world, we can't be happy in India. We must feel pain for each other, and that pain will get us closer. Today, we have several problems, but when people would join hands, there won't be a single problem. The best part of my country is that youth have started taking responsibilities in making the world a better place, that's why I'm here today.

RDS: How will you relate development and educational program in Kashmir?

SM: I would say that development and education should be in equilibrium, with education being the priority. Development can only happen when you have education. This can be understood in a way that we need alphabets to even spell development. It's really hard to think of development if we are not pushing our kids for education. If today we develop two schools, they in return it will give us infinite ideas and ways for sustainable development. Need to place priority for education first. Everything can wait but not education.

RDS: Are you satisfied with the educational policies of the union and state government with respect to Kashmir?

SM: Unfortunately, not! The big problem here in the valley is that everything is being ignored including education, to safeguard the vote banks. Government is nourishing ignorance in many forms. Like incompetent government teachers. So many people are holding a good position in the education department which they don't deserve. Recently, a teacher, who was in service for 16 years, was sacked for providing fake documents at the time of recruitment. Such cases are really heartbreaking. She ruined those 16 years of our students. This is just one example from many such cases. And the other problem is few people are taking advantage and making profits out of education, and authorities seem to be helpless. If we want a good India, we must prioritize education, why not turn India into an education hub, so that people from America and Europe come here to learn. That would be the best tribute to the people who sacrificed their lives for this country. They wanted India to lead the world.

RDS: If you ever get an opportunity to make education policies for the valley then how will you improve the system?

SM: It will be like a dream coming true.

I will keep education first in all aspects. Free quality education to every child till college. Easy access to education. Home-oriented education. Giving students a proper protocol to live their dream job in the system for a day to encourage them to pursue their goals actively. And will definitely make sure that education takes them close to the traditions and cultures of the nation. Will provide e-library in every locality and vicinity mentors. High placement chance for students belonging to government schools. Will make it mandatory for the school staff and officers to enroll their children in government schools. Constitute senior citizens and youth councils as pressure groups. Exchange programs with different countries. Providing education to differently abled children will be one of the priorities. Exempt of grade system.

Will try to showcase that education holds power to rescue all of us from the current issues. Will develop universities like Harvard here in the valley. Making it sure that all the other policies are education friendly. Will make education a non-profit service. Will restrict the area of students of primary level travelling taking care of their health. Will bring equality in the schools so that children of carpenters or casual labors open their lunch boxes with those from the privileged section of the society. If we want to live in the dream nation, we must crave for it now.

RDS: Education is the only weapon that can help us improve the condition of the valley. Do you agree with this? Also, what's your message to the youth who are getting involved in stone pelting?

SM: Indeed! I am a firm believer that education holds power to have an impact on things. There are always better ways and options that one can choose to get things done.

RDS: In your opinion what is the biggest challenge for Kashmiri youths?

SM: Insatiability in the structure of the system. Nobody is ready to hug them, to listen to their problem and issues. They always find it hard to get access to the system.

RDS: Who is your role model and what is your goal and what you want to achieve in your life?

SM: It was my childhood dream to help the people around, and I shall continue it to the limit of my endurance. Sufferings and problems of people are the biggest source of motivation for me. Every suffering inspires me and boosts me to work more for my people. I even get many good opportunities outside to work and study, but I opted to be here only. So that I can remain close to the problem of people, no matter if I don't get successful, but I'm chasing on the ground for a better future. I want to bring smiles to the faces of people, each face inspiring me to go more beyond to make more smiles.

RDS: What kind of Kashmir you want to see?

SM: A prosperous, full of positivity and possibility. Where social and Human rights are maintained in every aspect. Where everyone can dream with no limits. Where I can revive the old memories with our Kashmiri Pundit brothers, like my ancestors. Where Hindus who migrated from the valley can come back.

RDS: Is there any way to resolve differences? What is your opinion about current political developments and government policies in Kashmir?

SM: Dialogue is the only way out to end the differences and disturbance. If we fail to initiate the same, we may lose more smiles, and in this way, we are inviting more difficult situations.

RDS: What is your message to the people of this country?

SM: Kashmiris are not enemies to anybody; they need to be heard. They always wanted India to prosper in every aspect. They feel pain on their side. Kashmiris want to hug you; they want you to sit with them for a cup of tea. They want to tell you that what is being propagated on the sidelines is not true. They want to tell you the truth. They always share higher regards for you because they believe you only hold the capacity to resolve their impediments.

Kindly press it hard on the system to listen to the common voices of Kashmiris. Please help us to end this difficult time. Kashmiris also want to smile.

Talk With Actress And Activist Gabriella Wright

"We need to listen to each other deeply and

patiently, so that we can hear the silence behind our

words."

Beautiful part of any conversation is that you have the opportunity to know about a personality and his/her opinion but when I got the opportunity to interact with Gabriella Wright, I believe that from this conversation, you can learn about Life, Mental Health, Loneliness and secret of happiness. When I interacted with Co-founder of 'Never Alone' global campaign and English-French actress, model, humanitarian and activist Gabriella Wright, she was stranger for me and when the whole world was talking about depression, mental health and suicide, this conversation with another stranger is interesting.

Raaz Dheeraj Sharma (RD): Our way of living is changing and has become different than usual for every individual during the pandemic. How are you spending your days during this difficult period?

Gabriella Wright (GW): I am recreating home at home. In other words, I am finding ways to experience inner peace at all times. It was very easy for me to escape and travel for work purposes, or for any other excuse. I had my portable inner home that allowed me to be everywhere and feel at home. The irony is now to experience my inner home in my physical home. I meditate daily, write, and try to be as helpful as possible to those in need, even if it's just by a phone call or deep intention.

RDS: COVID-19 is not only affecting our physical health, but also our mental health, and people are still not ready to discuss mental illness. What are your views on corona and its effects on mental health?

GW: The tsunami of a pending mental health crisis is yet to come. We have dived into the deepest pandemic of our times with COVID-19 – it is questioning our state of existence and impermanence, and we are experiencing our own uncertainty and inner instability, which can only result in, if not taken care of, a deep scar of loneliness leading to depression and constant anxiety.

RDS: People are spending this lockdown period in self-introspection and giving themselves time to understand the meaning and purpose of life. What is the best way to understand the meaning of life?

GW: I think the best way to understand the meaning of life is by experiencing our connectedness. The beautiful side-effect of COVID-19 is that all over the world, we are experiencing the same feeling of helplessness. The virus is uncontrollable, and just like life, we cannot control life; but we can witness life, we can witness how we all want the same thing in life, and this is the experience of *Love* — through tender actions and the beauty of sharing presence with each other.

The meaning of life is to be an embodiment of 'love in action'. We have this precious human body; how can we value our lives and enhance our roles? I truly believe that if we can be *Love*, we shall experience not only our life differently, but even our view of reality differently. We shall be able to carry out our *dharma* with ease, and realize that the true purpose of life and meaning is to experience each other's presence and alleviate each other's suffering.

We are in a new era of communication, and technology is only to be more invasive and present in our lives. The real question is: why do we feel the need to present ourselves to the world of internet in a certain way?

RDS: Share with us something about your 'Never Alone' Project.

GW: 'Never Alone' is a global mental health and mental well-being movement I've co-created with Dr Deepak Chopra and Poonacha Machaiah. We decided that the campaign was much needed after realizing that every 40 seconds someone dies by suicide in the world. There is deeper suffering in this world and it is the basis of our relationship with this reality. We are in a deep need to change the narrative of mental health and destigmatize need for mental health so that we can help one another with practical ways to ease our relationship with one another and the lives we live.

During COVID, we organized a free three-day global mental health summit with over 105 speakers to help the community with practical tools to help one through these times. The speakers included Deepak Chopra, Patrick Kennedy and Russel Brand among others, who gave practical views and tools for us to navigate our own worlds during these times. It is still free and online on demand. Please use these resources at *www.neveralonesummit.live*.

RDS: In the era of digitalization, despite of having so many online friends and followers, why are people still alone? Is there any difference between loneliness and being alone?

GW: I would need a whole life to answer this question, there are several things to look at this question. First of all, we are in a new era of communication, and technology is only to be more invasive and present in our lives. The real question is: why do we feel the need to present ourselves to the world of internet in a certain way?, why do we need to show our shadows instead of our true selves? and why are we pushed to be artificial and believe the layers of illusion that people show as a collective on internet and social media?

The answer is in the questions of why we feel so insecure, and why does the illusion of having a following make us feel less lonely. Loneliness is a deep divide within, a deep sense of separation with our true self, our loved ones and the sense of reality. It is a deep alienation from within to our extended life. Being alone is experiencing our true self in our body, and finding peace in our infinite selves and our infinite nature, as we are truly a reflection of one another. Why our movement is called 'Never Alone' is because when we go deep within and become the human explorers of our own self. We experience a deeper connection that goes beyond our physical form, and our physical intersection with people and places. We experience a deep relationship that becomes the most important relationship of all, the relationship to our infinite nature, our own consciousness that is intrinsically the connection to all of us.

RDS: As per WHO, close to 800,000 people take their own life in the world every year. Where is the problem? Is losing human touch and connection the biggest problem?

GW: If I had the answer, I would have brought out my magic wand and extended my wish for all of us to heal immediately. There are several factors for this problem, but the most important factor is related to the deep up-rootedness we experience with who we are, our self-identity, self-image layered with overwhelming emotional conditions, and also mental illness. There is never one reason. We are multi-dimensional beings with 'diversity' as the essence of our true nature. I do feel that because of the extreme lockdowns all over the world, we are experiencing and realizing that we are more isolated than we thought we were. The extreme is the isolation in our minds. We need to listen to each other deeply and patiently, so that we can hear the silence behind our words.

RDS: You have been to Asian countries including India and Nepal. What kind of similarities did you observe between the Orient and the Western cultures?

GW: The only similarity is that we are humans walking on this earth, and we all want is safety, a home and experiencing love. The Western culture is laced with an urgency of productivity, and this sense of consumerism is unfortunately pervading everywhere. My favorite countries are Nepal and India. Why? Because here, time is slower, strangers are kinder, and there is a deep sense of worship and offering to a greater source than one's own life. The fact that there are prayers and incense constantly burning at almost every corner in Kathmandu is so beautiful, but also so calming. It's just magical. The sense of worshiping the nature is much more prominent in Asian cultures. Rituals that surpass our own 'self' and being of service are the greatest gift, which Asian cultures can lead and inspire the West to do more of.

RDS: Nature is a beautiful gift of God. Are humans becoming the biggest enemy of the Nature?

GW: Humans do not realize the precious gift that we walk on every day. Nepal is a beautiful witness and the womb of the grand chain of the Himalayas. I have never seen such beauty in my life. I bow down to such presence, because in my eyes it is the gift from God and every mountain, valley, lake and ocean is the constant offering we are given to survive with. We must not take it for granted. It would be a shame to pollute our mountains and rivers with plastic and other pollutants. At the end of the day, we are killing our own selves with the intake of micro plastics that are almost present in all packaged water or food items. We must see that everything in Nature is inter-dependent. We are not separate from nature, rather we *are the nature*.

RDS: Black Lives Matter is trending all over the world. Now some people are saying that this protest is discriminatory as All Lives Matter. What is your

response? Why are people becoming violent instead of promoting peace and humanity?

GW: There are several notions here. First of all, we are experiencing a huge economic crisis. Violence comes from frustration and a lack of means. Where I live here in the USA, most protests have been peaceful and supportive to all communities, but the media wants to underline the violence.

My response is simple. In most western countries, unfortunately, we have very deep systemic racism engrained in our institutions, our governments and our ways of creating our society. We didn't have the courage to change these systems since colonialism, which has brought out a nature of dominance in all places of the world.

We must always support those in need, question our privileges, and find peaceful ways to demonstrate and truly change our inner views. Global change comes from individual change, and no government or institution can give you that power. The power is within, the zest and thrill for the life you want to live comes from you. Policies and laws shall change if enough people become conscious at an individual level and deliberately.

RDS: What do you enjoy the most, acting or activism? According to you, which is the best movie?

GW: I love both! My life is entangled with both activism and acting. Earlier in my career, I was trying different things, roles and media. Obviously, having an acting career is good to get a platform where you can voice your opinion and raise awareness. I can definitely say that had I not been an actress, I would have been working in international politics or with the UN.

I have a deep sense of service, in a way where I truly feel, what else is there to do anyway? It's better to help people than just sit around and do nothing. I am a working mother. I was able to sustain a humanitarian activity all those years and also be an explorer. In my own way, I live a perfect life. I believe my best movie is yet to come. The final version of my film *I am Never*

Alone will be released hopefully by end of this year, and *Hitman Bodyguard 2*, a fun action film you might enjoy, will be out in August 2021.

RDS: We all have this perception that those in this glamorous world are often alone and depressed. What are your views on that?

GW: Some are and some are not. The truth is that money and castles can't buy you happiness. This is written in every scripture, every religion and every tradition. Material and wealth can help but it's not the way to enlightenment or liberation from suffering. We can all experience loneliness no matter what our 'status' is. Glamour is an illusion like everything else. As Shakespeare said,

"All the world's a stage,
And all the men and women merely players;
They have their exits and their entrances;
And one man in his time plays many parts,"

We have to go beyond our identities. Remember that this life is a stage and we are all actors in this dream. Let's awaken from the suffering together.

113

THANK YOU

WE WILL MEET IN ANOTHER JOURNEY